OCEAN STAR

EXPRESS

To William Cohen. M.H.

For Linda and Rebecca. P.S.

This edition produced for The Book People Ltd, Hall Wood Avenue, Haydock, St Helens WA11 9UL

First published in hardback in Great Britain by HarperCollins Publishers Ltd in 2001
First published in paperback by Collins Picture Books in 2002

3 5 7 9 10 8 6 4 2   ISBN: 0 00 770805 X

Collins Picture Books is an imprint of the Children's Division, part of HarperCollins Publishers Ltd.

Text copyright © Mark Haddon 2001   Illustrations copyright © Peter Sutton 2001

The HarperCollins website address is: www.fireandwater.com

Manufactured in Thailand for Imago

OCEAN STAR EXPRESS

Mark Haddon

Illustrated by Peter Sutton

TED SMART

This summer, Joe and Mum and Dad are spending two weeks by the seaside at the Ocean Star Hotel.

For five whole days the sky is bright blue and the air is warm as toast. Dad teaches Joe to do the crawl.

Joe rides the helter-skelter on the pier with Mum. They fish for crabs, play crazy golf and order knickerbocker glories in the Mermaid Tearooms.

Then the fog rolls in. Waves thunder on the misty beach and rain comes down in buckets. Joe watches water running down the window pane and thinks about his friends and toys and wishes he was still at home.

The hotel's owner, Mr Robertson, appears.

"You must be bored," he says. "I'll tell you what ... Let's take a journey round the world."

"But that's impossible," says Joe.

"You go and ask your Dad if you can come," says Mr Robertson, "and tell him we'll be back in time for tea."

They go upstairs until they reach the landing at the top.

"Where now?" asks Joe.

"Just one more flight," says Mr Robertson. He opens up a ceiling hatch and shiny metal steps slide down.

"You first," he says.

They clamber up into the dark. The loft is black as night. Above his head a thousand, tiny stars begin to twinkle. He hears a distant chug-chug-chug and sees a tiny light approaching through the dark.

The stars begin to fade away.
The sun comes up, and stretched
around him is the largest train
set he has ever seen.

He watches as the Ocean Star Express comes steaming down the valley to the station underneath his nose where a hundred model people wait.

Carefully, they pick the people up and put them in the carriages, then watch the train move off. It hoots and crawls across the river, past factories and farms and woods and disappears behind the hill.

"You made all this?" asks Joe.

"I did," says Mr Robertson. "But wait … You haven't seen the best of it. Let's find out where the Ocean Star Express is going next."

Squeezing through a hole, they come out in a second room. The train is roaring through a range of snow-capped mountains as they sparkle in the sun. The waterfalls are frozen. There are pine trees and a solitary moose.

"You press that button," whispers Mr Robertson.

Joe presses it. A string of little cable cars start moving, taking skiers up the slopes. The train steams by and vanishes into a forest.

"Come on," says Mr Robertson, "there's more."

They crawl into another room.

A blazing, yellow sun is painted on the ceiling.

There are camels, pyramids and palms.

Joe and Mr Robertson bend down and
blow to make a sandstorm, and the train
snakes on into the rolling dunes.

They duck and wriggle through another hole and come out in a fourth room. There are rocks and beaches and an ocean full of real water. Joe dips his fingers in and twenty fishing boats start rocking on the waves he makes. A lighthouse winks, the train honks twice and roars into a tunnel through the cliff.

One last squeeze and they are home. A church bell chimes. Brakes hiss. The train pulls up. They take the tiny people out and let them stretch their tired legs.

Before they leave the attic, Mr Robertson gets out a cardboard box. He digs around inside and finds a model of a little boy.

"Let's make him look like you," he says. They take out paints and brushes and they give him Joe's blue jeans and Joe's white jumper and Joe's blond hair. They sit him on the station bench. They put a tiny suitcase by his feet. They put a tiny ice cream in his hand.

"Now, every time I come up here," says Mr Robertson, "I'll put you on the train and you can travel round the world again."

They go downstairs. The rain has stopped. The sun is shining. And it keeps on shining. Mum and Dad and Joe build castles on the beach. They visit the aquarium and ride on the bumper cars.

And soon the holiday is at an end. They pack their bags and say goodbye to Mr Robertson and drive away.

Back at home Joe lies in bed and as he falls asleep he starts to dream about the Ocean Star Express. He hears a distant chug-chug-chug and sees a tiny light approaching through the dark.

His bed becomes a station bench. The rucked-up duvet is a mountain range. His nightlight is the moon. And he is tiny now. There is a tiny suitcase by his feet and in his hands a tiny ice-cream cone.

The train slows down. Joe climbs aboard and settles down. The whistle blows. The wheels start to turn. The carriage rumbles and the Ocean Star Express pulls out into the star-filled night.